胖打 與 Panda & Polar Bear

北七熊 日記

3

愛 的 大 冒 險

Panda & Polar Bear 3：Adventure of Love

韋采伶、大衛‧霍金森 著

謹以此書
獻給我們的家人

本書及作者簡介

這是大衛 (Dave Hodgkinson) 與采伶 (Louise Wei) 的半自傳故事，兩個人分別在英國與台灣長大，卻一見鍾情，由於時常在彼此身上感受到不同文化的有趣異同點，於是將這些情節畫成了漫畫，自 2012 年 7 月開始在網路上發表，受到來自世界各地讀者的支持與好評。

官方網站：pandaandpolarbear.com
中文臉書：胖打與北七熊日記
　　　　　PandaAndPolarBearTW

譯者簡介

蘇渝婷 (Jill Su)，身兼多職的譯者，熱愛翻譯，迷戀動物，生活無時無刻都環繞著翻譯與動物，就像呼吸般自然。

聯絡方式：a1481a@hotmail.com

施百俊 屏東大學文化創意產業學系教授、台客武俠創始人

2016下半年我第一次造訪英國。那時脫歐公投剛過，實在無法待在陰鬱的倫敦，於是老婆聯絡上了 Louise，想過去她家住幾天。她一口氣就答應了。轉了幾趟火車，終於來到威爾斯。遠遠就看到胖打與北七熊站在出口等我們。沒錯，就是他們兩個，和書裡畫的一樣。

北七熊 David 是這麼打招呼的，喂，先說好，威爾斯這是另一個完全不同的國家，一邊一國，不要搞錯啊！（註）接下來的幾天，兩夫妻就帶著我們去逛皇家花園、礁石海岸、火車長征、羅馬浴場……簡直累趴。北七熊自己倒是頂自在，反正餓了就吃、渴了就喝、喝了就醉；開心就把胖打抓來親兩下、不爽就開罵。而胖打呢？則忙著做設計賺錢、導航、付帳、打招呼……繞著北七熊轉。

後來我去到牛頓的蘋果樹下，回憶這段有趣的旅程才頓悟：一顆恆星，一顆行星──胖打與北七熊兩人的太陽系裡，運行著宇宙的終極規律，那就是愛的萬有引力。

註：英國由四個構成國組成，分別為英格蘭、蘇格蘭、威爾斯和北愛爾蘭。

自　序

渴望將美好的瞬間留作永恆 —— 這也許是所有相愛的人們共同的願望吧！對我和大衛來說，「胖打與北七熊」就是將這份回憶保存下來的方式。充滿著回憶的瑣事，就像柴米油鹽一樣使生活有了滋味。

歌頌「愛」的作品很多，而我們希望透過兩隻截然不同的熊，來呈現出愛的寬容。藉由面對生活中的荒謬與矛盾，來理解愛的意義。希望大家會喜歡，也願胖打與北七熊能帶給大家快樂與溫暖！

本書得以順利出版，非常感謝好友慕姿、BJ 老師、Jill 的大力幫忙，更謝謝編輯柚子、秀威資訊以及讀者們的支持。如本書有任何錯誤之處，是我們的疏忽與不足，請包涵並不吝指正，謝謝！祝福各位！

CONTESTS

※ 為了閱讀方便，本漫畫的中文與英文並非完全對照，是以故事整體的語意通達為準翻譯。

嗯⋯⋯⋯⋯⋯⋯⋯

Mmmmm..............

喂！妳也過太爽！快工作！
Stop bloody enjoying yourself!

🐾 禮拜一的心情
Monday

妳應該把自己聞
蕁麻，刺到鼻子的事畫出來。
You should draw Panda
sniffing stinging nettle.

妳應該把我
生病吵著要喝茶的事畫出來。
You should draw grumpy Polar Bear
demanding tea.

妳應該把自己躲在
被窩裡逃避現實的事畫出來。
You should draw Panda
being useless.

不要。
No.

（鼻音）

不要。
No.

不要。
No.

……我放棄。
...... I give up.

耶！！！
Yeah!!!

成功的祕訣
The Secret to Success

我們買了一台車！
We bought a car!

嘿⋯我覺得應該
還需要一台行車記錄器！
Hey... I think we should get
a car camera!

不行，這樣我就慘了。
No, I'd get into trouble.

麻煩
Trouble

…因此當人魚公主發現
王子已經愛上了新來的女孩時，

...So when the princess
found out that the prince had
fallen in love with the new girl,

她心碎了…

her heart was broken...

她投入大海，化為了泡沫…

She turned into bubbles
and drifted away with the sea…

…所以這就是為什麼我們
怎麼找都找不到舊的導航了。

And this is why we can't
find our old satnav.

這樣啊…
RIGHT...

新的汽車導航
New Satnav

熊話故事
Beary Tales

ZZZzz

哈…
Ahh...

哈啾！
CHU!!!

妳把我也吵醒了！
You woke me up!

你不是在開車嗎？！
Weren't you suppose to be driving?!

🐾 把我也吵醒了
You Woke Me Up

在北七熊心中，酒吧是最安全的避難所。

去酒吧
To The Pub

警鈴大作
Alarming

 吃小籠包？沒那麼簡單
One Does Not Simply Eat Dumplings

註：Nom Nom 是享受美食時大快朵頤的滿足聲音。

全素美食節會後趴
Vegan Fest After Party

正義魔熊
Being Right

給阿基米德一個支點，
他就會撐起整個地球；
給胖打一個樓梯，
她就會去拜訪北七熊。
Give Archimedes a place to stand on, and he will move the Earth.
Give Panda a ladder to stand on, she'll visit Polar Bear.

熊的世界觀 🐾
Bear Geography

熊熊星球
Planet Of The Bears

天啊！我真不敢相信我們天天
一起吃飯出門，可是卻只有你得感冒！我真沒看過
這麼會生病的熊！等你好了我一定要多帶你去運動，
還有多吃水果！你一定要更注意身體了啦！今年你都不知道
第幾次感冒了，反而我上次感冒都不知道幾年前了！你看看！
現在感覺好點沒？剛剛吃的藥有效果了嗎？生病不好受對不對？
不要嫌我囉唆，我講這麼多都是為你好！而且我們搬來這裡這麼久
還沒有去跟家庭醫師登記呢！看你這次還有什麼藉口…

Again? I can't believe that you got cold and I didn't, it must be your immune system, we need to go to the gym more!! Also eat more fruit! You really need to watch out for your health you know, do you have any idea how many times you've been ill last year? And I didn't! We eat and do everything together! How do you feel now? Has the drug kicked in? You don't want to get more of that believe me!I'm only saying this for your own good! Can't believe we haven't sign up to a doctor... You don't even need to pay for it! What's your excuse this time?......

是的…
別再…碎碎念…啦！
Yes... and stop nagging...!

等一下…我現在
才知道你的肚子裡還有
一個袋子可以藏熱水瓶…?!
Wait, Is that a
Pouch on your belly?

生病記
You Have A Pouch On Your Belly?

幸福小馬
Lucky Horse

倫敦奧運開幕的那天⋯
一隻熊把手機搞丟了，另一隻連回家的路都找不到。

On the opening night of London Olympics...
One lost her phone and the other one simply got lost.

那一晚
That Night

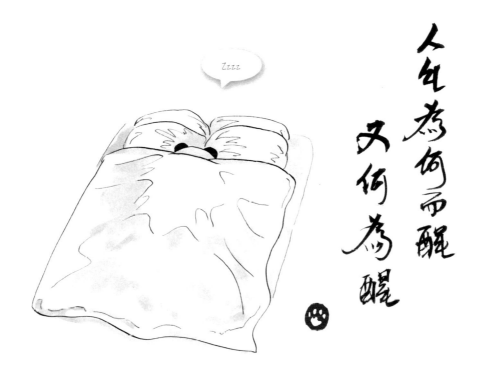

人生為何而醒
又何為醒

Why did I get out of the bed this morning
When I was very much happier snoring?

睡覺哲學家
Philosopher's Sleep

將每一天都看作是自己的最後一日，那麼隔天早晨醒來就可以…
Live each day as if it's your last, so the next day you can be…

重生了！耶！
Reincarnated! Yeah!

吵死了…！
Shut... up...!!

重生
Reincarnated

去動物園的前一天 🐾
Day Before Zoo

你好…請問熊貓
與北極熊在哪裡？
Hello...Can you tell me where
Pandas and Polar Bears
are please?

哎呀…真抱歉！
我們這裡沒有…
Awww...I'm so sorry, we don't
have them!

現在不就有了嘛。
YOU DO NOW.

🐾 **去動物園的那天**
Day At The Zoo

本站是倫敦動物園。
This stop is London Zoo.

他剛剛是說：
「我們去倫敦吃湯圓」嗎？
Did he just say:
We stop and have some soup?

我以為只有我才會
把話聽錯成吃的東西！
That's something I would say!

…都怪我們在一起太久了…
......We've been together for too long.

你已經徹底被我同化了。
Yeah, you've been Pandalised.

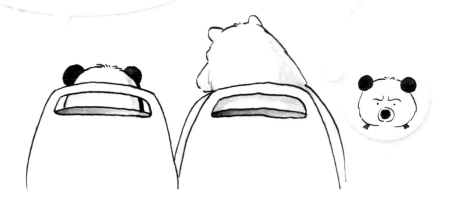

被同化了
Pandalised

1 準備 Loading

2 開車 Driving

3 抵達 Arriving

4 喝茶 Tea

🐾 音樂祭行程
Metal Festival Protocol

就算工作也要很搖滾
Hard At Work

註：史提夫・范是美國著名搖滾吉他手。

🐾 如何把音樂祭搞得很尷尬
How To Be Awkward In Festivals

你睏了嗎？
Are You Asleep

熊出沒羅浮宮
Bear Feet In The Louvre

到底為什麼要挑
熱浪來襲時來巴黎……？
Why did we come to Paris when there's a heat wave?

因為我想吃法國料理嘛！
Because my foodar told me to!

那你說食物在哪裡？
So where's the food?

那裡。
That way.

快！冰淇淋！
I want ice cream!

……

熱到融化的熊
Bearly Melted

淨空！
Clear!

🐾 隱藏功能
Undocumented Feature

胖打和好朋友貝貝熊一起去看「哈利波特」電影片場的展覽。
Panda and her friend little Beh-r went to "The Making Of Harry Potter" WB Studio Tour.

如果我忍不住要買魔杖的話，一定要阻止我喔！
Stop me if I try to buy a wand ok?

天啊！
妳真的 Hold 得住嗎？
Gosh! How can you resist!

佛地魔的墓碑
在美麗的豔陽下
in a sunny day

海格的摩托車

才剛玩回來
現在又想去了對不對？
You're thinking about going there again, aren't you?

／ + ／ = ∥
兩隻魔杖 = 一組筷子！
2 Wands = Chopsticks!

我是很實際的，
相信我，我只買實用的束西。
Oh I'm just thinking about practical things, I assure you.

霍格華茲啤酒杯
Hogwarts Pint Glass →

隱藏功能 2
Undocumented Feature 2

室內天氣超級冷
Raining Indoors

現在有很多人喜歡帶自己的玩具熊到處旅行、拍照……
Many people like bringing their bears to places and take photo with them.

無聊死了，
拍好了沒？
I'm bored! Is it
done yet?

不知道耶……
Dunno.

我們也很喜歡。
We like it too.

一、二、三、起司
Say Cheese!

一定還有下一次
We'll Be Back

好了，
我們的退休金就靠妳了！
Look, our pension depends on YOU!

等等……我應該是
受保護的動物才對呀 ?!
Wait... Weren't Pandas suppose
to be protected?

等不及變有錢人
Can't Wait To Be Rich

憤怒之筷
Chopsticks Of Fury

胖打是怎麼來的呢？
The Birth Of Panda

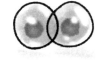

一個細胞，
One Cell,

分裂成兩個細胞，
Two cells,

…胖打！
Panda!

胖打的誕生
The Birth Of Panda

日本 *Japan*

紐西蘭 *New Zealand*

中國 *China*

俄國 *Russia*

蘇格蘭 *Scotland*

南極 *South Pole*

假如北七熊是在其他地方長大的
If Polar Bear Was Adopted By Other Places

在家種熊貓 Growing your own Pandas

北七熊的追尋 🐾
Finally I Can Poop

根本沒有冰塊，怎麼裝進桶子啦！
Got no ice to put in mah bucket.

🐾 冰桶挑戰
Ice Bucket Challenge

你知道嗎？
北極現在開了新的海豹
送貨服務耶！以後你就
不用擔心浮冰會消失了！
這上面說他們很環保喔…
Check this out...
A new Seal Delivery service in North Pole!
Now you don't need to worry about the
disappearing sea ice! They say it's very
environmental friendly...

不，謝了。
我一直都很不環保。
No thanks, I'm Environmentally
Hostile.

不環保
Environmentally Hostile

🐾 **熊注意**
Please Don't Piss Off This Bear

牌子掛上去第三天了，
他開始想「難道我很受歡迎？」…
Day 3, he starts to think he's popular.

熊注意 2
Please Don't Piss Off This Bear 2

差點嚇得我毛都掉光了。
I nearly jumped out of my fur.

🐾 脫毛記
Nearly Jump Out Of My Fur

衛生與安全
Health & Safety

家具大風吹遊戲
Tetris Time

我們去參觀煤礦博物館⋯ *We went to a coal mine tour⋯*

礦坑裡的熊
Bear In Mine

就是這樣我才擔心…
That's exactly what I'm worried about...

安啦！
我很會畫亞洲人的臉喔！
Relax, I know how to draw Asians!

月餅臉
Asian Moon Face

被獨角獸踢死

Kicked to death by a Unicorn

被菠菜罐頭噎死

Choked to death with a tin of spinach

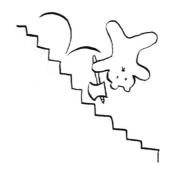

下樓梯不小心摔死

Broke his neck by falling down the stairs

可惡！
我又死了！

F*ck!! I Died!
Again!

…有意思。

...Fascinating.

被小貓咬死

...And bitten to death by a kitten

手機勇者
Brave Phone Warrior

60

我們從英格蘭搬到威爾斯後經過了一個月……
After spending a month moving from England to
Wales for Polar Bear's new job…

現在我們搬到這裡來，
妳還是學學開車的好。
Now that we moved here, you need to learn
to drive.

好吧。
...OK.

就由我負責教妳。
And I'll teach you.

等等！…
Wait...

新的大冒險
A New Adventure

我們的新冒險就從這裡展開…！
註：L 牌是學習駕照。

And A New Adventure starts here...!
*L plate means Learner's Driving license in UK

「她的威爾斯語進步很多喔。」
註：威爾斯是噴火龍的國度嘛…
"Her Welsh is really coming along."
*Wales is known as the Land of the Dragons.

🐾 胖打練習說威爾斯語
Panda Practising Welsh

Love Underlined

談情説愛

註：熊在樹林裡便便（*Bear shit in the woods*）是一句英文諺語，用來形容理所當然的事情。

熊在樹林裡做什麼？
What Do Bears Do In The Woods

靠左行駛，音同左邊有熊。

左邊有熊
Bear Left

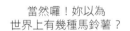 大的跟小的
Large Ones And Small Ones

* 註：*Hallucination* 是幻覺，*Halloumi* 是一種起司，煎過很好吃。

起司的幻覺
Halloumination

好香！是月桂樹。
Nice! It's a bay tree.

還好不是棵吳三桂樹，
As opposed to a Michael
Bay Tree

…不然現在清兵就打來了。
...which will just explode.

吳三桂樹
Michael Bay Tree

像熊文字
Bearly Easy Mandarin

他應該會猜
我們在講什麼吧！

I think he must be guessing
what we're talking
about.

我跟朋友
聊天時，他都乖乖滑手機。

He always looks at his phone patiently
when I chat with friends
in Mandarin.

我記得他
有一次說「中文字好像
喝醉在紙上亂跑的蜘蛛⋯」

I remember he said Chinese characters
are like drunk spiders walking
on paper...

所謂中文是場陰謀
Mandarin Conspiracy

人生在世不稱意，
明朝散髮弄扁舟。

李白

For tho' from out our bourne of Time and Place
The flood may bear me far,
I hope to see my Pilot face to face
When I have crost the bar.
"Crossing the Bar"   by Alfred Tennyson

弄扁舟
Bear Me Far

One Day
愛 的 紀 念

今天是愛爾蘭國慶日！不過，只是一個喝酒的藉口啦…

聖帕特理克節
St. Patrick's Day

國際**女人**節 🐾
International Women's Day

備註：May the 4th（五月四日）與 May the force（願原力）同音，影迷因此將本日定為星際大戰日。

🐾 慶祝星際大戰日
May The 4th Be With You

如果蘇格蘭獨立的話，
我還可以早餐吃蘇格蘭燕麥粥嗎？
Can I still have porridge for breakfast after
Scotland gets independence?

……不行。
……No.

那蘇格蘭奶油酥呢？
What about shortbread?

不行。
No.

蘇格蘭折耳貓？
Scottish Fold Cat?

當早餐嗎？不行。
For breakfast?
No.

威士忌？
…可以。

Whisky?
..Yes.

哈吉斯？＊
Haggis?

不行。
No.

梅爾吉勃遜
之英雄本色？＊
Braveheart?

天啊！
絕對免談！
GOD NO!

＊註一：哈吉斯又稱爲「肉餡羊肚」，是蘇格蘭的國菜。
＊註二：出身英格蘭的北七熊對這部片有著本能的抗拒…

獨立還是不獨立？
Yes Or No?

我剛才發現
已經十月了！(October)
I just realised it's
October!

你不會變身成
八爪熊吧？(Octobear)
You are not gonna turn
into an Octo-Bear,
are you?

才不會咧！
那是什麼鬼？
NO! What the hell
is that?!

好吧！
OK!

傻傻的胖打。
Silly Panda.

八爪熊
Octo-Bear

不給糖就搗蛋
Trick Or Treat

備註：英國傳統的聖誕布丁上桌前會先淋上白蘭地並點火。

🐾 傳統的由來
Where The Tradition Came From

一隻「好」熊
A Good Bear

🐾 **聖誕盆栽**
Christmas Bonsai

*註：在檞寄生底下親吻是聖誕節的習俗。

佳節傳統
Holiday Tradition

聖誕老熊熊
Santa Claws

1945
邱吉爾首相
早晨在床上辦公
Churchill working from bed

2017
北七熊
早晨在床上推文
Polar Bear tweeting from bed

我真是了不起。
I'm Great.

我真是註定
要當一隻了不起的熊。
I'm destined to
be Great.

註定要當個偉人 🐾
Destined To Be Great

新年新計畫

1. 多做瑜珈。*Do more yoga.*

Zzzzz...

這個姿勢很標準！
Great posture!

🐾 新年新計畫
New Year's Resolution

新年快樂之要說吉祥話
Happy Lunar New Year!

國際北七熊節
Grumpy International Polar Bear Day

The End

不過癮想看更多？

立刻上臉書：胖打與北七熊日記

感動的理由
Reasons To Cry For

醀生活14　PE0114

胖打與北七熊日記3：愛的大冒險
Panda & Polar Bear 3 : Adventure of Love

作者／韋采伶、大衛‧霍金森
翻譯／蘇渝婷
責任編輯／徐佑驊
圖文排版／蔡瑋筠
封面設計／蔡瑋筠

出版策劃／醀出版
製作發行／秀威資訊科技股份有限公司
114 台北市內湖區瑞光路76巷65號1樓
電話：+886-2-2796-3638
傳真：+886-2-2796-1377
服務信箱：service@showwe.com.tw
http://www.showwe.com.tw

郵政劃撥／19563868
戶名：秀威資訊科技股份有限公司
展售門市／國家書店【松江門市】
104 台北市中山區松江路209號1樓
電話：+886-2-2518-0207
傳真：+886-2-2518-0778

網路訂購／秀威網路書店：http://www.bodbooks.com.tw
　　　　　國家網路書店：http://www.govbooks.com.tw
法律顧問／毛國樑　律師

總經銷／聯合發行股份有限公司
地址：231新北市新店區寶橋路235巷6弄6號4樓
電話：+886-2-2917-8022
傳真：+886-2-2915-6275

出版日期／2017年08月　定價／350元
ISBN／978-986-445-215-6

國家圖書館出版品預行編目

胖打與北七熊日記3：愛的大冒險

　　　　　韋采伶, 大衛.霍金森作 ; 蘇渝婷翻譯.

-- 臺北市 : 釀出版, 2017.08

面 ;　　　　　　　　公分. -- (釀生活 ; 14)

BOD版　　　　ISBN 978-986-445-215-6(平裝)

855　　　　　　　　　　　106012107

讀者回函卡

感謝您購買本書，為提升服務品質，請填妥以下資料，將讀者回函卡直接寄回或傳真本公司，收到您的寶貴意見後，我們會收藏記錄及檢討，謝謝！

如您需要了解本公司最新出版書目、購書優惠或企劃活動，歡迎您上網查詢或下載相關資料：

http:// www.showwe.com.tw

您購買的書名：_____

出生日期：_____年_____月_____日

學歷：□高中 (含) 以下　　□大專　　□研究所 (含) 以上

職業：□製造業　□金融業　□資訊業　□軍警　□傳播業　□自由業　□服務業　□公務員　□教職
　　　□學生　□家管　□其它_____

購書地點：□網路書店　□實體書店　□書展　□郵購　□贈閱　□其他

您從何得知本書的消息？

　　□網路書店　□實體書店　□網路搜尋　□電子報　□書訊　□雜誌　□傳播媒體　□親友推薦

　　□網站推薦　□部落格　□其他_____

您對本書的評價：（請填代號　1.非常滿意　2.滿意　3.尚可　4.再改進）

　　封面設計_____　版面編排_____　內容_____　文／譯筆_____　價格_____

讀完書後您覺得：

　　□很有收穫　□有收穫　□收穫不多　□沒收穫

對我們的建議：_____

_____

_____

_____

11466
台北市內湖區瑞光路 76 巷 65 號 1 樓

秀威資訊科技股份有限公司　　收

BOD 數位出版事業部

....

（請沿線對折寄回，謝謝！）

姓　　名：＿＿＿＿＿＿＿＿＿＿＿＿＿　年齡：＿＿＿＿＿　性別：□女　□男

郵遞區號：□□□□□

地　　址：＿＿＿＿＿＿＿＿＿＿＿＿＿＿＿＿＿＿＿＿＿＿＿＿＿＿＿＿＿

聯絡電話：(日) ＿＿＿＿＿＿＿＿＿＿＿＿　(夜) ＿＿＿＿＿＿＿＿＿＿＿＿

E-mail：＿＿＿＿＿＿＿＿＿＿＿＿＿＿＿＿＿＿＿＿＿＿＿＿＿＿＿＿＿